With Thanks To

Daniel Easton
Benjamin Thomsett
Callum Gwinnell
Callum Newman
Chelsea Roberts
Rafe Dance
Joshua Milton

For Donating Some Words

This is a simple book by a simple man. I thought it would be entertaining to people if I was to take words and have a pop at figuring out what they mean and use them in what I then consider to be context.

A little bit about me, I am a supposedly clever member of society, I have managed to get through university, I got finished college, did reasonably well at school and show off my artistic streak with taxidermy! However I know very little about lots of things. Usually when I speak people tend to laugh or smirk, it isn't because I sound retarded it's just because I say apparently stupid things.

So you might laugh, you might not. You might get so sick of this that you stop at page 5 and leave it next to the toilet for the rest of the time you live in your flat. Who knows, but someone will enjoy it I'm just pretty sure it won't be me.

Enjoy the pictures.

V

Abstemiousness

Noun [ab-stem-ee-ous-nuss]

A part of the mind which generates art and abstract ideas, it bridges the gap between the conscious and subconscious areas of the mind. It pulls subconscious thoughts into your conscious thoughts.

Example – When the artist was asked what gave her the idea to project the times from around the world onto corresponding faces of natives living in them time zones she responded with a shrug of the shoulders. It is presumed her abstemiousness brought together the synonyms of faces whilst looking at a world map.

Acrocyanosis

Noun [Ack-roe-cyan-oh-sis]

A debilitating illness from which the victims skin pigment quickly takes on a light blue pigment.

Example – Lucy had been swimming in the reservoir a little bit too much over the summer. Her mother had warned her the water wasn't reflecting the sky, but Lucy didn't listen. Poor Lucy she's caught acrocyanosis, but on the bright side she'd never had a nickname before – now all her friends introduce her as 'Mystique'.

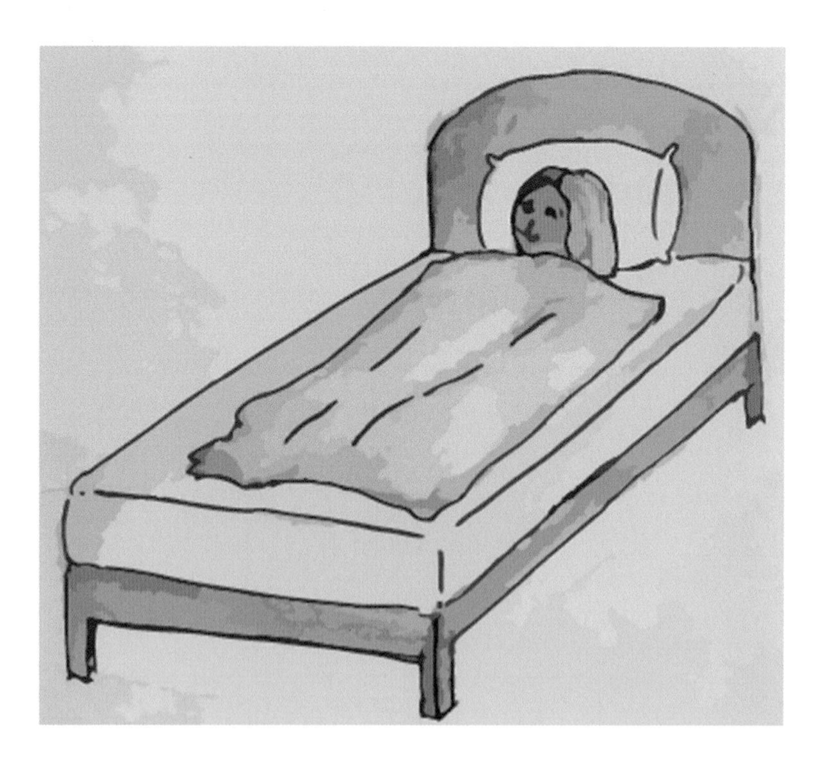

Agrostologist

Noun [ag-ro-stol-lo-jist]

A person of science, specialised in the study and prediction of anger. Using somebody's star sign the scientist is able to provide information on what is most likely to annoy a person.

Example – The police didn't believe Gary was capable of a beheading and his character references backed this up. But the detective had a hunch about Gary, so he hired the world renowned agrostologist, Conroy Fischer to weigh in on the case. Professor Fischer discovered Gary was earlier denied a simple bank withdrawal, however due to being a Sagittarius this wasn't likely to be the cause. Conroy stated that it was the number 87 bus arriving fifteen minutes late that triggered the incident as people born under this star sign tend to be extremely agitated by their own lateness.

Ameliorate
Verb [A-meal-ore-ate]

1. Handling a dangerous situation without violence.

2. Reacting calmly to a threatening presence.

Example - I was able to ameliorate when the bloke pulled out his knife, I'm actually that good at ameliorating that he bought me a pint later that day.

IX

Anachronistic

Noun [an-a-kron-ist-ick]

A person who is purposely late to everything – holds a total disregard for time.

Example – Gainor is late to every single thing she attends she is a total anachronist.

Anadiplosis

Noun [an-a-di-plos-sis]

A six legged deep sea creature encased in a hard shell.

Example – Due to the increase of radiation in the South Pacific it is theorised the Arthropod populations of the sea floor have grown exponentially, with the Anadiplosis reaching sizes matching that of an estate car.

Atelectasis

Noun [ah-tel-eck-tay-sis]

The state both a phone and its user are in after attempting to answer a call from a 'one beller'. The caller has already hung up in anticipation of the recipient ringing back, but the natural action of answering the phone continues.

Example – Stacy was in atelectasis after Mark one belled her. She was so flustered by his actions she rang back when she came to. Win-win for mark, he gets to go on a date and he didn't have to pay for the call!

Blandishment

Verb   [Blan-dish-munt]

Making a space boring.

Example – Marie's need for blandishment forced her to burn the posters on her son's bedroom wall.

Brobdingnag

Noun [brob-di-nag] (Gaelic)

Originally a Gaelic term, used to name a dangerous and intimidating creature with an unknown identity. Nowadays used to describe an unknown assailant of violent crime.

Example –

1) "The Brobdingnag has taken another victim, all that remained was the rib cage, we need to capture this beast! "

2) He was attacked by a drunken Brobdingnag in the early hours of the morning.

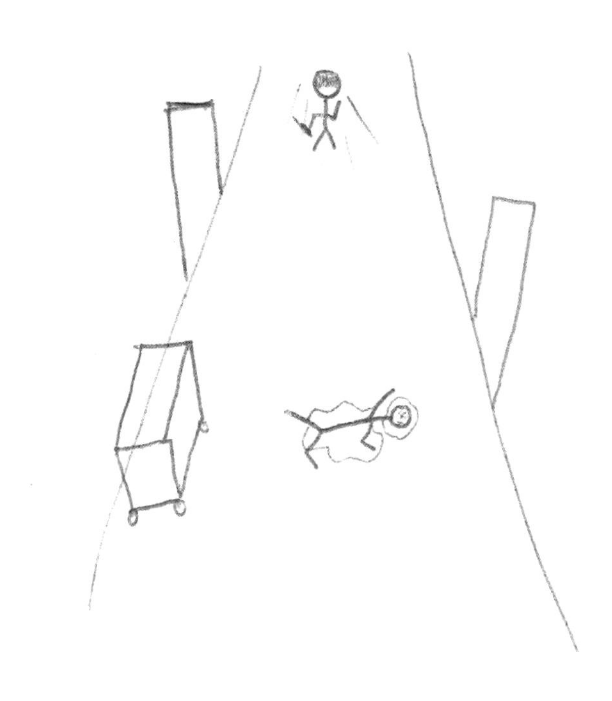

Buckjumper

Noun [buk-jum-pur]

A hunter involved in a deer cull.

Example – Buckjumpers tend to meet up to swap stories on the last night of a cull. They'll have a venison feast, using the meat hung from the first kill.

Callipygian

Noun [Cal-ip-ee-gee-un]

1. A person who makes leg supports for the world of medicine.

2. A person who manufactures or aides in the manufacture of surveying equipment.

Example –

1. Joanne was mighty disappointed when she opened her seemingly small parcel from the callipygian. After all she is 6ft4.

2. Captain Jo Anne was very confused by the arrival of a 3 foot box the morning before she set off on her around the world adventure.

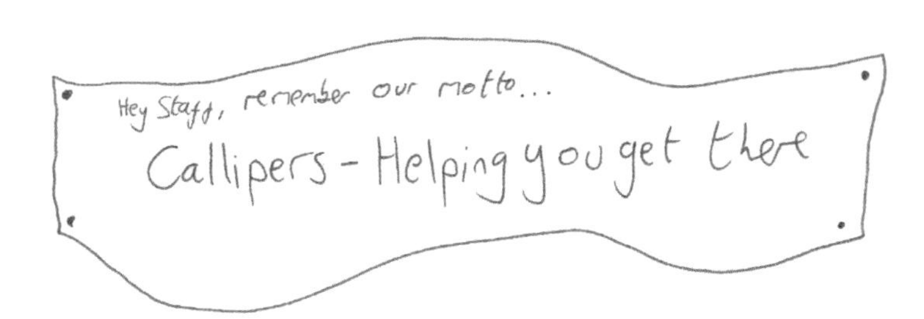

Catercornerways

Noun [kate-er-corn-er-ways]

A commercial chef, using self-taught methods to speed up cooking and food preparation activities.

Example – When Ludvig set off the smoke alarms and shattered the windows of the kitchen, the owners immediately acted to fire him. But when he explained himself they discovered he was “speed roasting a turkey” using his homemade concoction of explosives. The owners were so impressed by Ludvig’s catercornerways that they put him in a transparent, sound proof room in the eating area, where Ludvig’s exploding poultry quickly became the star attraction.

XVII

Circumscription

Noun [sir-kem-scrip-shun]

The specific waver a doctor signs along with a patient/parent/guardian that defers all responsibility regarding mistakes surrounding a circumcision.

Example – Gene was on the bus when he realised he had forgotten his circumscription, Dr. Falschtick was never going to perform the procedure without it.

Commensalism

Adjective [Com-men-sal-in-ul-ism]

The general notion of starting a new project and the associated feeling.

Example – The team were rearing to go on their new build, the labourers were ready with their shovels, the demolition guys were heading to their next job and the foreman was shouting out orders. Commensalism was sweeping the site!

XIX

Condign

Verb [con-dine]

Being outwardly negative of a situation, but inwardly happy and accepting of the situation.

Example – Telling your wife the marijuana smokers next door annoy you, but secretly you share an occasional joint with them over the fence.

XX

Consanguinity

Noun [con-san-gwin-it-ee]

The records held by health officials regarding a person's mental health deterioration over time. It is used as a reference to prescribe medication to patients and also to see if the patient is hiding something or faking ailments.

Example – The doctor read over Malcolm's consanguinity with prejudice as he had heard a blonde lad had been selling Valium outside the local corner shop. He could see little to no effects from taking such a strong dose, however his proof was only theoretical, Dr Yunther decided if he can't stop young Malcolm from dealing the prescribed medication he could at least deter him by prescribing a much lower dose "this will surely stop him from making money" thought the doctor as he handed the prescription over to Malcolm, grimacing.

XXI

Contemporaneous

Adjective [con-temp-ore-ayne-ee-uss]

The act of purposely being spontaneous, pretending to be spontaneous by already thinking through an action yet the act is perceived as spontaneous by onlookers.

Example – As the group stepped off the coach Joseph announced he fancied going to the red light district. Everyone agreed this was a great idea and followed as it was bound to be more enjoyable than the science museum. Joseph led the group directly there, nobody in the group even questioned how he knew the way through the Belgian streets. Joseph was pleased, no one suspected him of booking ahead. His contemporaneous decision had been completely overlooked.

Corpulent

Noun   [cor-you-lunt]

Being a part of a large team or squadron, military term. A meeting of similarly ranked individuals.

Example – Janes corpulent always loses football games at the barracks but they ace the shooting range.

XXIII

Cycloserine

Noun [Si-clo-sir-een]

The name of the creatures eating each other's tails - often included in alchemic drawings.

Example –The winged beast and snake creature become one by chewing each other's tails, this is known as the Cycloserine in alchemic terms. The Cycloserine is often depicted in front of a tree.

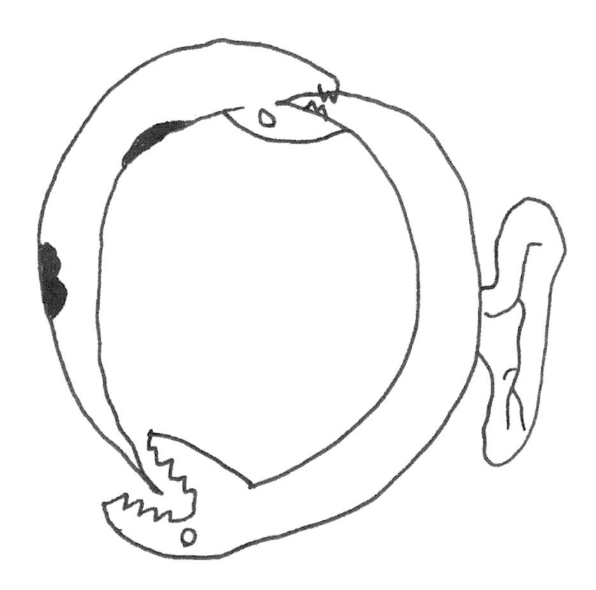

XXIV

Defenestration

Verb [dee-fen-iss-stray-shun]

To metaphorically dismantle a person's creation, specifically artists.

Example – Dale wasn't mentally ready for the brutal defenestration of the critics.

Desalination

Verb [Dee-sal-in-ay-shun]

The act of removing salt from a liquid solution, often achieved by boiling the liquid and allowing the condensation to catch in a tube and reform as a salt-less solution in another container.

Example – The desalination was a success Lord Steven Roids and his wife Emma will be able to remain hydrated on the final leg of their sea voyage.

XXVI

Disseminate

Noun [Diss-em-in-ate]

The day when you deconstruct your Christmas decorations, specifically the day you dismantle your tree, but is commonly used to describe the entire day.

Example – When Pete was 6 years old he suffered his worst dissemination when his parents argued whilst placing the boxes in the loft. That argument spiralled into the release of years of tension and eventually led to his parents' divorce. He still blames himself for his family falling apart.

Dramaturgical

Noun [Dram-at-err-ji-cull]

A sham operation. A medical procedure which is entirely fictitious, widely practical and still reportedly beneficial to the patient.

Example – Whilst lying in the hospital bed Sven was told by Dr Jones that the surgery was dramaturgical, Sven was confused at first because he had witnessed the camera work on the screen in theatre. Dr Jones explained it was a previous recording and the only thing real was the anaesthetic and the stitches.

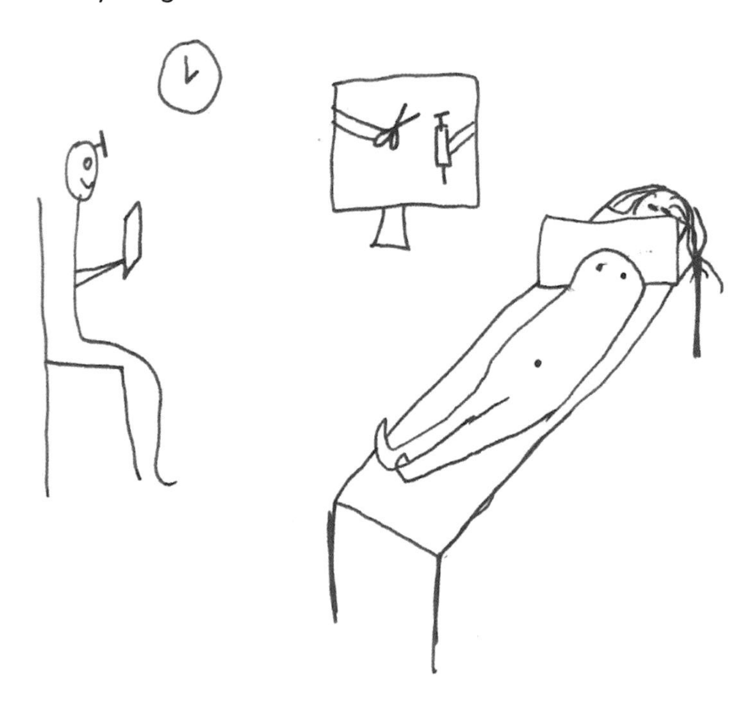

XXVIII

Echidnophaga

Verb [eck-id-no-fay-ger]

To create spikes.

Example – Egbert couldn't wait to teach his eldest grandson how to echidnophaga. It was a family trade, his grandfather had taught him how to echidnophaga at a similar age. In the Swanson family it was a coming of age ritual, and the first spike manufactured would be cause for great celebration.

Edificial

Adjective [ed-iff-ish-ul]

After a newspaper article has been edited to manipulate the truth in order to create more interest in the story.

Example – Although the interviewee said that the home intruder climbed in through an open window the edificial stated the perpetrator smashed the window.

Effervescence

Adjective [eff-er-vess-un-ss]

The sense of hard work going into somebody else's work.

Example – I can really feel his effervescence when I look at his spread sheets.

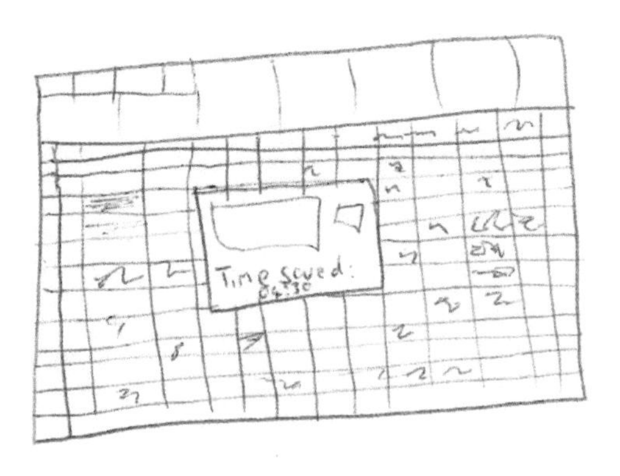

XXXI

Emaciated

Verb [em-ay-see-ate-id]

When an altar boy/girl is dressed and blessed before they begin their role at a mass.

Example – Stacey's parents were proud of their daughter earning the role of a choir girl at their local church; Dale's parents were proud too, however they were very worried about him being emaciated every morning by the priest.

XXXII

Endomorphism

Verb [End-oh-morf-is-um]

Actively increasing the temperature of a room.

Example – The endomorphism began with Steven turning the thermostat to transform the room into a Sahara–like condition.

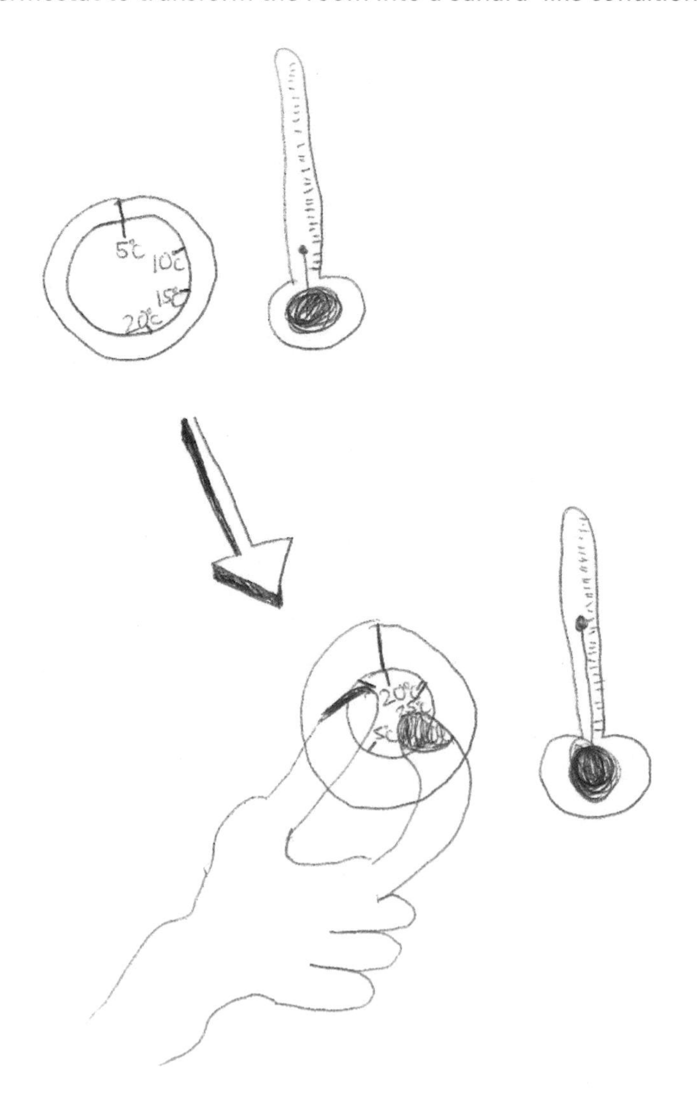

XXXIII

Enjambement

Noun [em-jam-ber-munt]

Unwarranted singing in public places, usually undertaken by intoxicated individuals.

Example – The enjambement really unsettled the other mourners at Anthony's wake.

XXXIV

Ephemeral

Adjective [Ef-em-ar-ul]

When a person observes from the corner of their eye, due to a smell or sound.

Example – He ephemerally acknowledged the chef from the clanging of the pans.

Equanimity

Noun [Eck-wa-nim-it-ee]

The moment of uncertainty when a horse race which is a photo finish.

Example – 'Hebrodonis' and 'Ferrodonk' ran such a close race, the equanimity created such an atmosphere until officials announced the victor; Terry had £50 on 'Ferrodonk' his Equanimeous state delayed his celebrations.

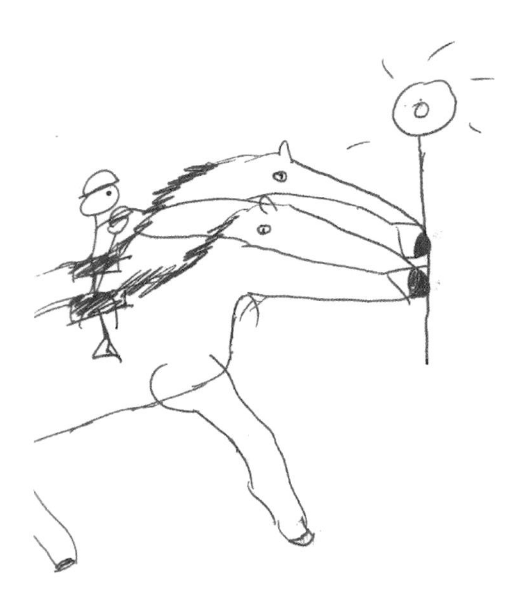

Eriocaulon

Noun [Err-ee-oh-call-on]

The sounds made by floorboards creaking in the night, the sound is often associated with stomach rumblings.

Example – Jason refused to spend another night alone in the manor he told Janet there was a hungry ghost roaming the halls. Janet sat him down with a cup of tea and explained about the phenomenon of eriocaulon in old houses.

Espouse

Noun [E-spow-sss]

The name of a virtual spouse.

Example – Anthony couldn't wait to go onto 'Dungeons, Trolls and Pixiedust' to tell his espouse, Annette, all about his day.

XXXVIII

Euouae

Exclamation [oi-you-ay]

A way of explaining your discontent towards somebody else's actions.

Example – {Carl's neighbour is hitting his dog in the garden} "Euouae, stop it!"

Exteroceptor

Noun [ex-ter-row-sep-ter]

A person who feels a compulsion to intercept the postman before they reach their property.

Example – Ibrahim was set in his ways, he was always used to his dog tearing up any letters he received, but now 15 years after the death of 'Rex' he is still an exteroceptor. He isn't causing any harm. In fact his postman will sometimes wait a little up the road until his door opens to humour Ibrahim.

Fascistic

Adjective [fas-sh-ist-ick]

Purposely having the appearance of a dictator or villain.

Example – James decided having a fascistic fringe would make him appear more serious at job interviews, but the cape hindered his chances.

XLI

Fastigiated
Noun [Fas-sti-gee-ate]

The process of artificially speeding up an incubation period of any seed or egg.

Example – If the eggs weren't being fastigiated in the sand the power outage would surely have delayed any attempt at repopulating the crocodile population.

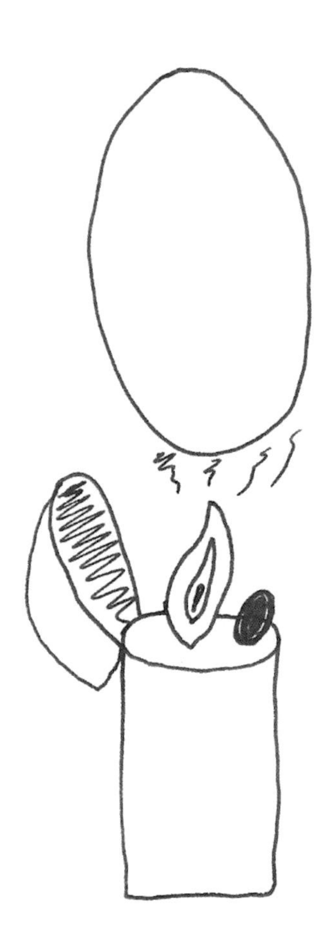

Flummery

Noun [Flum-mer-ee]

Breaking bad news to children, missing out upsetting details for the child's benefit.

Example – After Dennis died his wife took their son aside and gave him a flummery, she told him his dad is dead. But he doesn't know he slowly bled out trapped under the steering wheel of his car.

Gerrymandering

Adjective [Je-ree-man-der-in]

A boring, mind numbing experience.

Example – The torture was horrendous, they tied her up, strapped her to a chair and proceeded to paint the walls and floor around her. They used cheap paint - the cheapest. The torturers were methodical in their work and doused the paint brushes in white spirit, when they left the room it is claimed that they played nursery rhymes on repeat for the next two days. The victim was quoted in the papers as saying "the combination of chemical fumes and constant threat of danger countered the gerrymandering nature of the torture".

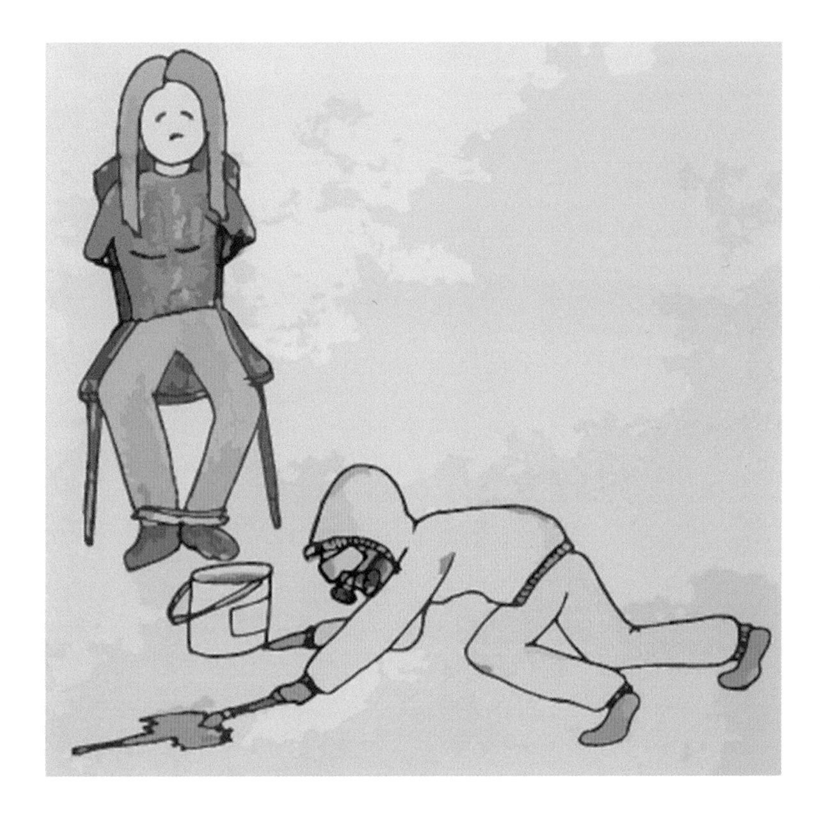

Gratuitous

Verb [grat-you-it-uh-ss]

Being prematurely and innately grateful for a concealed gift – even though you've no idea what is inside the wrapping.

Example – Her gratuitous nature was obvious to the party goers as they pointed out her massive grin whilst she stared at the pile of presents on the pub table.

Heterogeneous

Noun [het-er-oh-jean-uh-ss]

The gene that makes people straight.

Example – Mr and Mr Frendrichson had intense blood tests as part of a scientific experiment and it was discovered they carry the heterogeneous, but it is recessive.

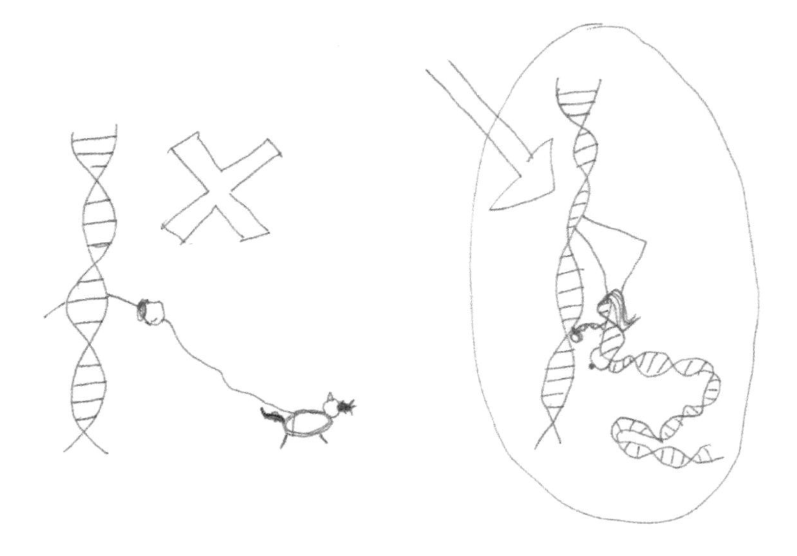

Immutable

Adjective [Im-mue-ta-bul]

A TV or radio show which is too good to turn down.

Example – Sarah had never laughed so hard in her life her eyes were squinting, her stomach was aching and her jaw was sore. The talk show was just immutable. Maybe it wasn't safe to be travelling 70mph but after explaining the reason why she had parked on the hard shoulder to the police officer, he understood and suggested recording it at home to listen to in a safe environment. Luckily she only got a caution.

Incontrovertible

Noun [In-con-trow-vert-a-bull]

An original concept for a car where, whilst driving, the body would stop away from the frame of the car and gets stored in the boot of the car. Exposing both driver and passengers.

Example – The first test run of the incontrovertible car ended in the death of the driver and the debris along the motorway caused delays for thousands of busy commuters.

Incumbent

Verb [In-cum-bnt]

1) To have room for more

2) Yet to be filled

Example –

1) Charlottes shopping trip ended with her approach to the till clutching the handles of her incumbent trolley.

2) The homeless gentleman searched his incumbent pocket hoping for a sandwich.

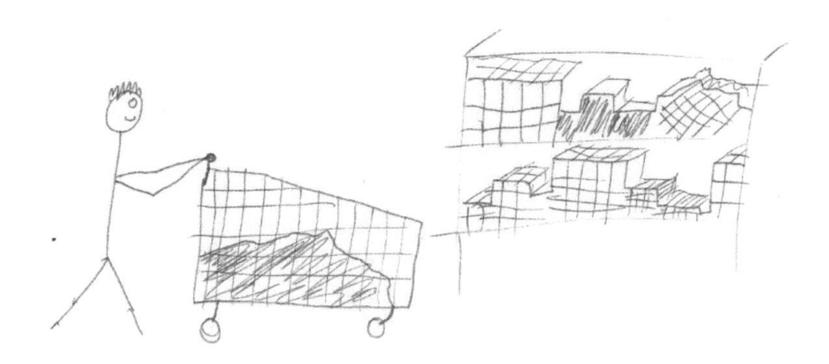

Ineffable

Adverb [in-eff-ab-ul]

When an argument is in a situation where swearing is not at all acceptable.

Example – When somebody offends you in front of your children and you want to stand your ground but not teach your child swear words – an ineffable situation.

Infinitesimal

Noun [In-fin-its-ee-mul]

Finding no way of resolving a problem, there seems many possibilities of how the problem may be resolved, but it remains impossible.

Example – "How am I going to load this van by myself, its infinitesimal. If I had another person helping me, or a forklift it'd be possible. If I wasn't in the middle of this muddy field I would be able to at least walk it over to the van."

Judicious

Verb [jew-dish-uss]

When a judge or magistrate believes a jury might be rigged.

Example – The hearing made Judge Hoogie judicious, he was sure he had seen the defendant talking to the foreman earlier that week.

Juxtaposition

Noun [ju-ck-sta-pos-si-shun]

The finishing places in competitions and tournaments between third and last.

Example – Although Harold never truly came last, he was always disheartened. Even though he rose through the juxtapositions he was always a failure in his father's eyes as he never earned a medal.

Lateritious
Noun [lat-er-ish-uss]

When somebody's guess is wrong, however the initial guess is close to the correct answer. Often expressed as "along the right lines"

Example – Harry was trying to learn the new computer software, but the button didn't do what he intended, but when he clicked the drop down menu he found the correct option.

LIV

Mellifluous

Noun [Mel-li-flu-ss]

Evil intentions with seemingly honest actions.

Example – The Trojan horse was a mellifluous act. A seemingly honest gift was given with the intention of the hidden army infiltrating and taking over.

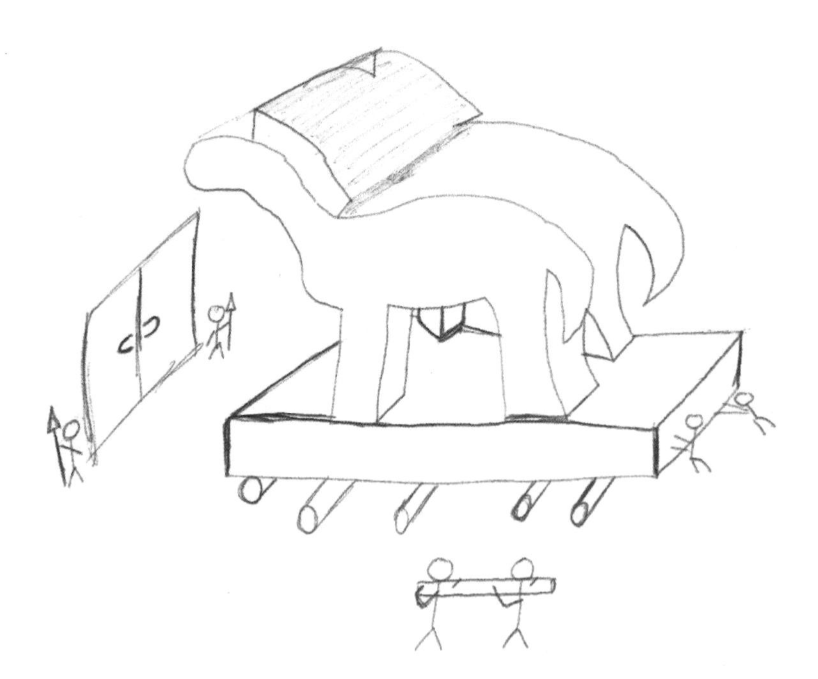

Nagelfluh

Verb [Nag-ul-flu]

To give somebody lots of jobs to the point where completion of the tasks is going to result in fatigue.

Example – [2:30pm] "Do the dishes, wash the cat, pluck the pheasants for tea, pick the children up from school and make sure you take Timmy for a haircut, re-carpet the stairs and plane the door so it fits into the doorframe easier. Oh and we need you to do it all before the evening news starts."

LVI

Pantisocracy

Noun [Pan-tee-sock-rass-ee]

When a woman convinces a man about something by seducing him.

Example – They had been debating all day trying to decide upon a holiday destination, but they both knew she was always in charge. Coming out of the bathroom wearing nothing but his favourite stockings she asked him again "Can we please go to Hull?" immediately he said "I can't wait to see the Humber". He was oblivious to her use of a casual pantisocracy.

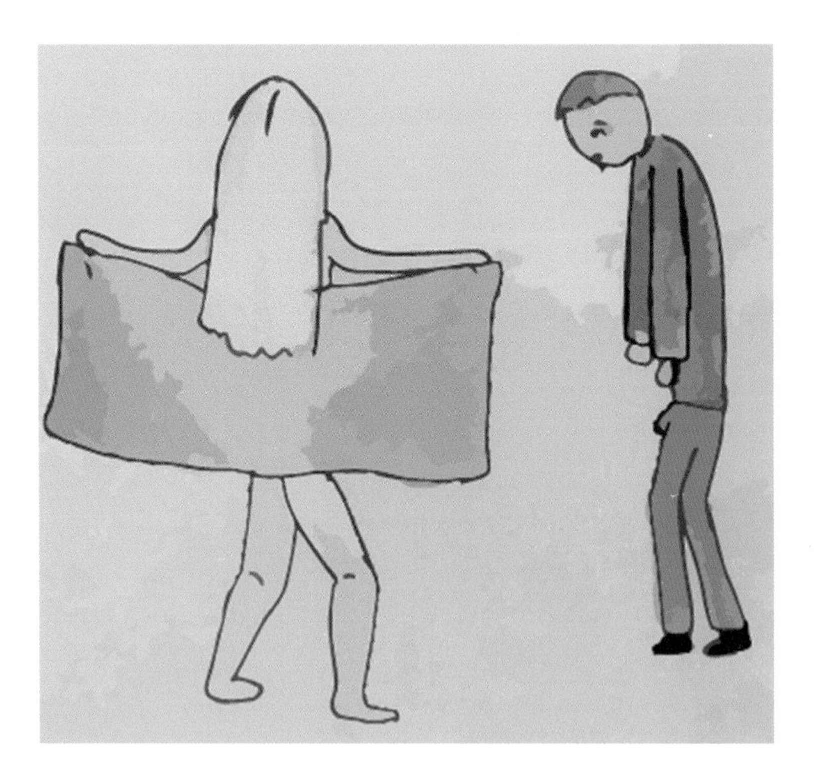

Paramecium

Noun [Para-mee-key-um]

The shared property of chemicals that will appear to replicate other substances by appropriating their qualities.

Example – When they discovered mixing Terbium in its gaseous state with Oxygen the researchers were dumbfounded when it appeared the amount of Oxygen present had doubled with the Terbium all but untraceable.

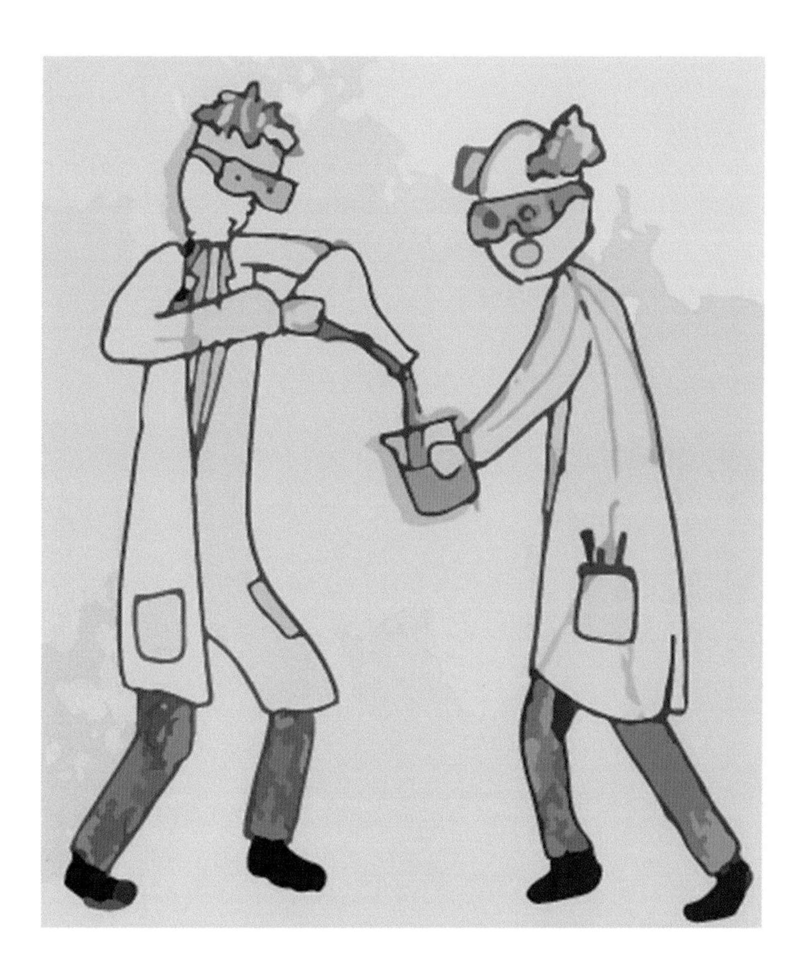

Pentlandite

Noun [Pent-lan-dite]

A person from a country which borders 5 other countries.

Example – Joanna was born in Belarus, so she has the right to call herself a Pentlandite.

LIX

Pneumonoultramicroscopicsilicovolcanokoniosis

Noun [new-mono-owl-tra-micro-scopic-siliko-volcano-coney-oh-sis]

The illness caused by a micro-organism which causes cold like symptoms that was originally found thriving within the hot lava conditions of active volcanos and geysers.

Example – He has swelling of the eyes, a strong cough and a small growth in his lungs, I know he regrets traveling to exotic locations since the doctor told him he's come down with a bit of the old pneumonoultramicroscopicsilicovolcanokoniosis.

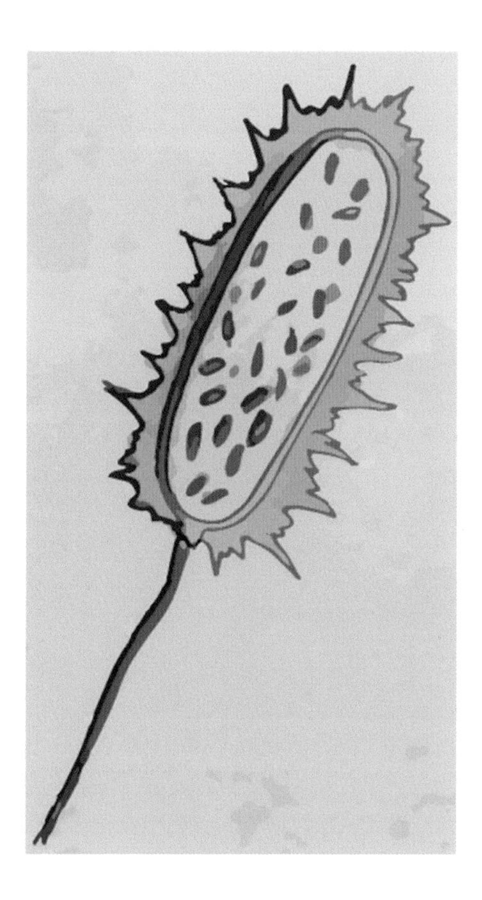

Polynomial

Noun [Polly-gnome-eel]

A collection of calendars. A group of more than 5 calendars, usually used by owners of greetings card shops and calendar collectors.

Example – My polynomial is coming along well, I've got cats from 2015, puppies of 2015 and fast cars calendar from every year since 1993.

Polyptoton

Noun [pol-ip-toe-ton]

A small frog that was hunted to extinction in the early 1400's for its oils to aid in the production of fabric dyes.

Example – The French army's uniform was so vibrant thanks to the Polyptoton oils.

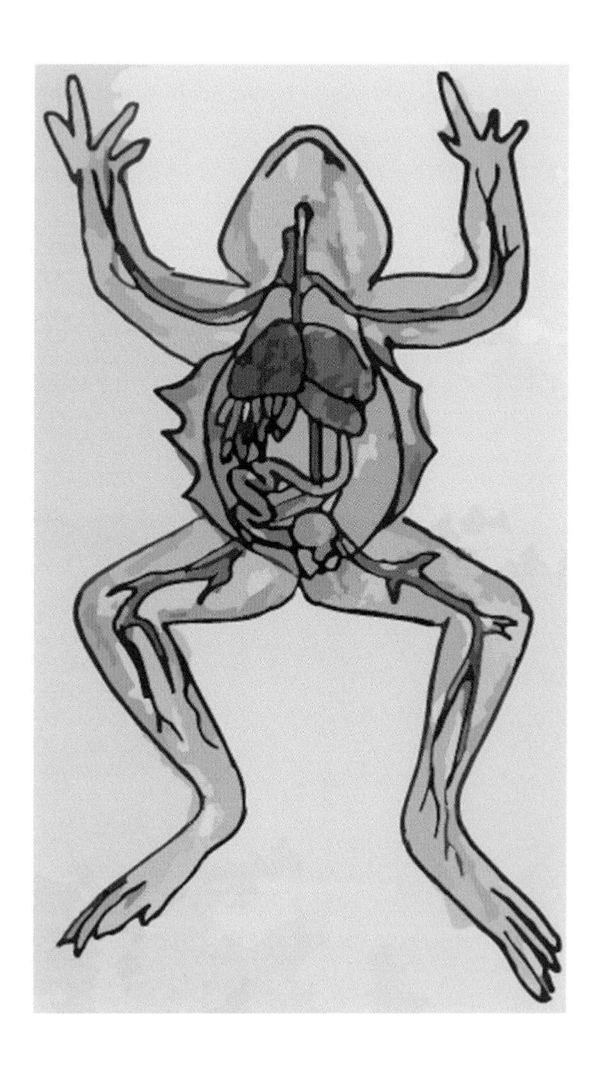

LXII

Praseodymium
Noun [pray-zz-od-im-ee-um]

The special recognition given to the intellectually inferior when it is apparent they have given it their full attention, yet still failed to accomplish the task.

Example – Mr Ghoulsin took note of young Pete's attempts at solving the equation, it had always been clear mathematics wasn't his forte. After scolding the class on an overall poor attempt at the work set he ordered young Pete to stay behind. It was here that Pete's life was turned around, after hearing the praseodymium from his teacher he knew that trying hard mattered in life and was certain as long as he tried everything would be OK.

LXIII

Precipitately

Adjective [Pr-cep-ee-tayt-lee]

Showing affection in long inconsistent bursts.

Example – James would precipitately give gifts and flowers to his lovers to hide his true actions, allowing him to carry on behind their backs with one another.

LXIV

Pulchritudinous

Adjective [pull-cher-ee-tud-in-house]

Foul smelling, a smell that makes you feel like the taste will stay in your throat.

Example – The smell of that old asparagus next to the window is pulchritudinous, I am not going to be able to eat for the rest of the day.

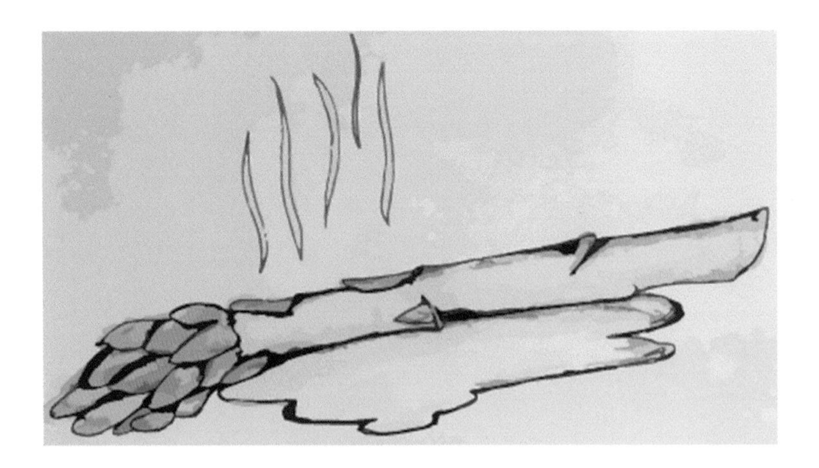

LXV

Repudiation

Verb [re-pew-dee-ay-shun]

To remove items that have been resting on a chair so that it may be sat on again.

Example – Those children of mine don't think about my bad back at all, they leave all sorts on that couch. But after a swift repudiation I was able to rest in front of the telly.

LXVI

Rotundity

Noun [Row-tun-ditty]

When baron land is converted into workable farm land, suitable for growing produce.

Example – Rotundity is part of the life cycle of farmland.

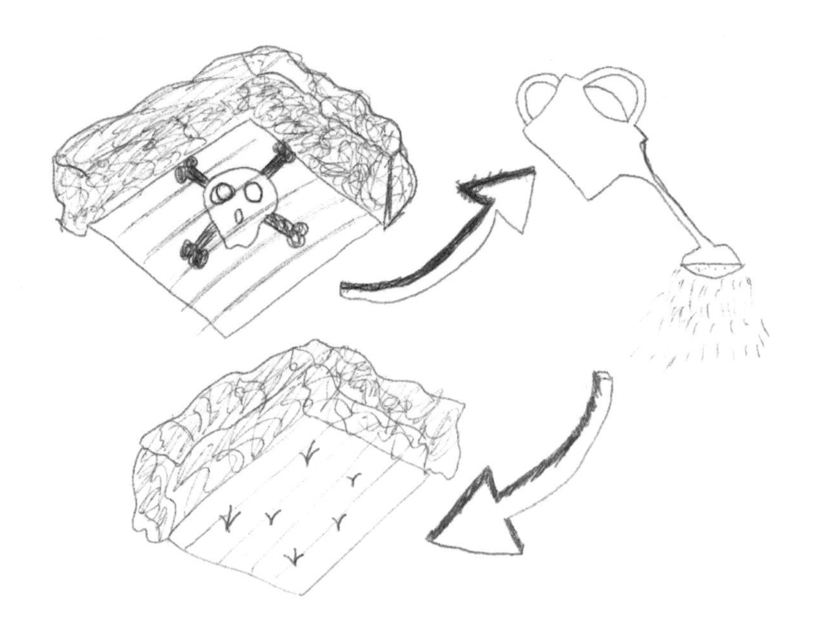

LXVII

Routinization

Noun [ru-tin-eye-zay-shun]

The initial steps to change and eventually destroy a country's culture by making them appropriate new daily rituals.

Example – After Colonel Dandy had secured ground over the border of Wales he ordered his troops to spray paint any welsh road signs so that only English words could be read. Wales was about to undergo a guerrilla routinization, the likes of which it had never seen.

Septuagenarian

Noun [Sept-you-agun-air-ee-un]

1. A member of an ancient race often in association with phallic monuments and the worship of staffs and sceptres held by their mythical deities.

2. A way of describing a tall structure.

Example – Gilbert told Sandra that the Washington Monument was positively Septuagenarian. Sandra replied by calling Gilbert out as a pervert as they began to reminisce on happier times.

LXIX

Sonorous
Noun [so-no-rus]

A high pitched sound wrongly associated with aquatic mammals, the origin of the sound is usually machinery.

Example – “Them dolphins were really noisy last night” said the orphan on the boat, “you idiot, no wonder your family disowned you, that was the generators on the lower deck – that’s called a sonorous noise”

LXX

Stramineously

Adjective [stra-min-ow-ss-lee]

Used to describe the juddered roofline when terraced houses go up a hill.

Example – The architect had spilt her coffee on her initial drawing of the new project, but she really liked how the roofline moved stramineously across the sky.

Streptococcus

Noun [strep-toe-co-cuss]

A family of insects with mandible like growths from the spine. They metamorphose in their 3rd month of life into a striped moth.

Example – It's my favourite time of the year, let's go to the hills and watch the Streptococcus hatch from their cocoons and take the sky.

Stultifying

Verb [Stul-ti-fy-ing]

To be left to sit for a long time, usually results in rotting.

Example – After a two week holiday James returned home to find his groceries stultifying in the fridge, the milk was particularly bad. The peppers had become soft, gooey and mouldy. He was particularly disheartened by the new found firmness of his birthday cake.

Superannuated

Noun [soup-err-an-you-ate-id]

The very rare leap year associated with the Earth's orbit is longer than 365¼ days.

Example – 2020 is predicted to be superannuated due to 2018's forecast 365½ day cycle.

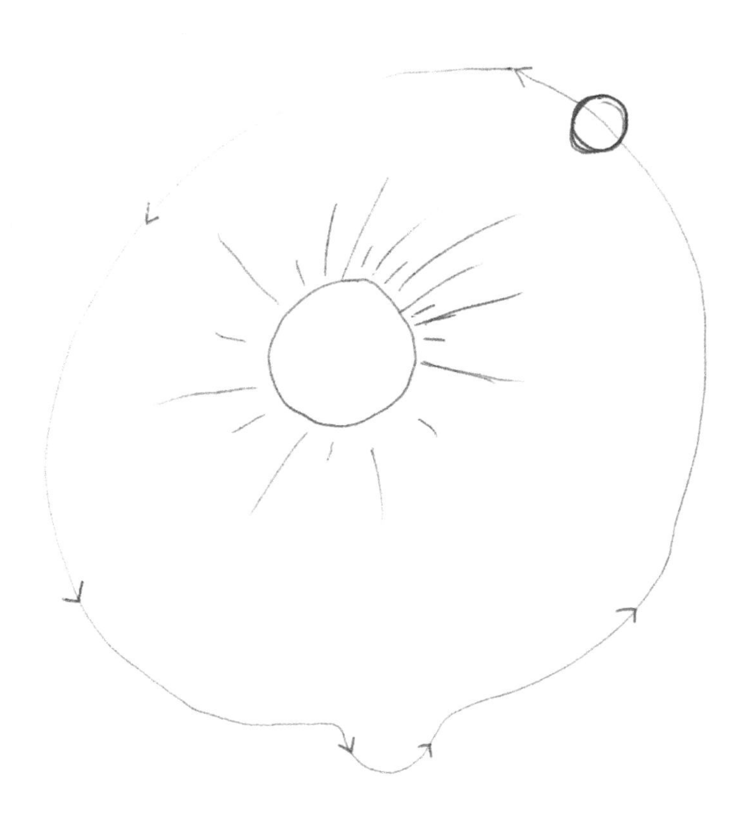

LXXIV

Superciliousness
Adjective [supe-er-sil-ee-uss-nuss]

Passing something along person to person.

Example – The labourer passed the brick to the next labourer by the van door who threw it to the lad on the wheelbarrow. They could empty a tonne pallet out of a van in 10 minutes between them. They had been inspired from listening to a radio show on the drive to the job where a caller talked about bringing up mucus. They figured they could impress the foreman by working in a superciliousness manner. And they were right, before they knew it they had increased productivity and received a pay rise.

LXXV

Supine

Adjective [sup-eye-un]

When something is a little more than satisfactory, marginally beyond expectations

Example – "I was expecting the car to kill me at 40mph but instead it has left me paralysed... how supine" thought the old man at the hospital.

Surrejoinder

Noun [sur-ri-join-da]

The bond between a child and their surrogate mother.

Example – Once a year Rita would meet Sophie and her children and revel in the fact Sophie's life had been successful, even though Rita had no part in raising Sophie, she knew she had made the right decision in agreeing to carry her in her womb. Surrejoinder is so powerful it kept Rita going through her final years, Sophie felt it too. As gratitude for making her life possible all those years ago, Sophie started to visit Rita more frequently to make her life more fulfilled. Despite Rita dying a spinster Sophie and her parents decided it was only fitting that Rita's epitaph read 'Mother, Grandmother, Friend'.

LXXVII

Syzygy

Noun [siz-er-gee]

A lesbian orgy.

Example – Tina, Georgina, Francine and Carol invited Sarah over for a syzygy.

Tessellation

Verb [Tess-a-lay-shun], to tessellate [tessel- eight]

The act of spinning an object around or causing something to spin at a very high speed.

Example – The tessellation of the Earth is what causes the 24 hour day and night cycle.

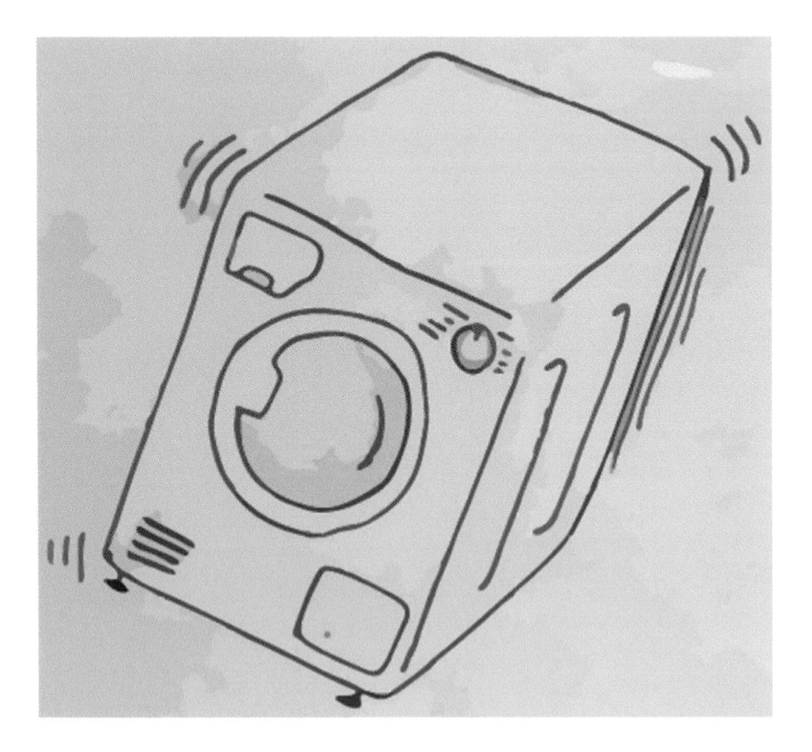

Thessalonica

Noun [thess-sal-on-ick-aa]

A modern twist on barber shop quartets, a band comprising of acoustic sounds produced within a hairdressing salon and the accompanying singing hairdressers.

Example – Charlotte, Rebecca and Matty were nervous before their first public performance at the North West Thessalonica Competition. Rebecca was only playing the broom but it was nice for her to feel involved. But the rest of the ensemble know Matty tends to come into his own on stage.

LXXX

Tutsan

Noun [T-ts-un]

Dissatisfied grumbling.

Example – Sanjeev's friend had pebble dashed his coffee on the living room rug, he knew his wife wasn't happy when Steve was saying goodbye to Sanjeev's wife as she merely responded with a look of distain and tutsan noises. Although he knew he had made a mistake Steve walked away making his own tutsan noises.

LXXXI

Unguiculate

Verb [un-goo-shu-late]

To remove unwanted matter from the sole of a shoe.

Example – "I don't care how urgently he needs medical attention, you're not coming on my new carpet until you have unguiculated" screamed Georges wife through the letter box.

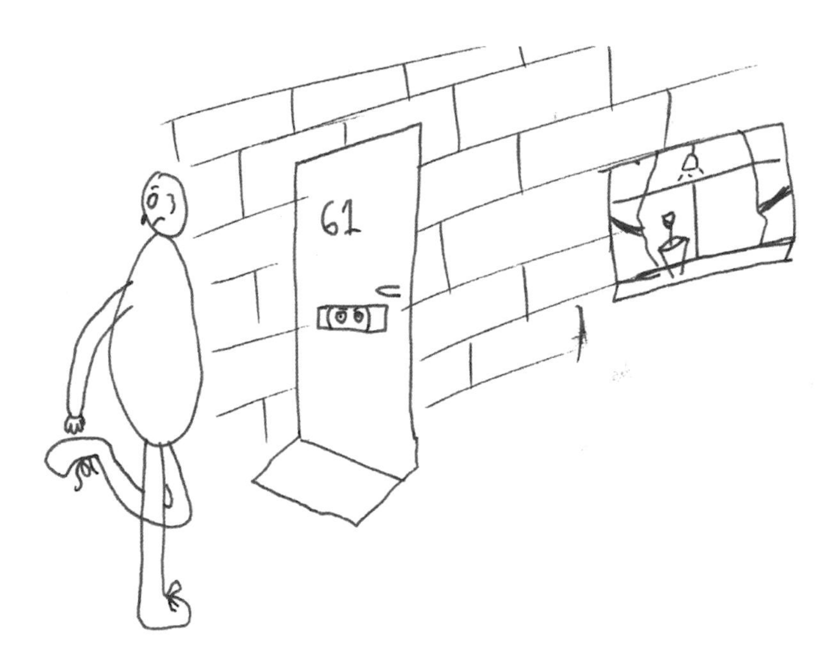

LXXXII

Verisimilitude

Noun [verr-issi-milli-chude]

The judgment of a products ability to have multiple uses. It is the scale their measured on.

Example – The new computer I bought rates high in verisimilitude, but the highest rating is the Swiss army knife.

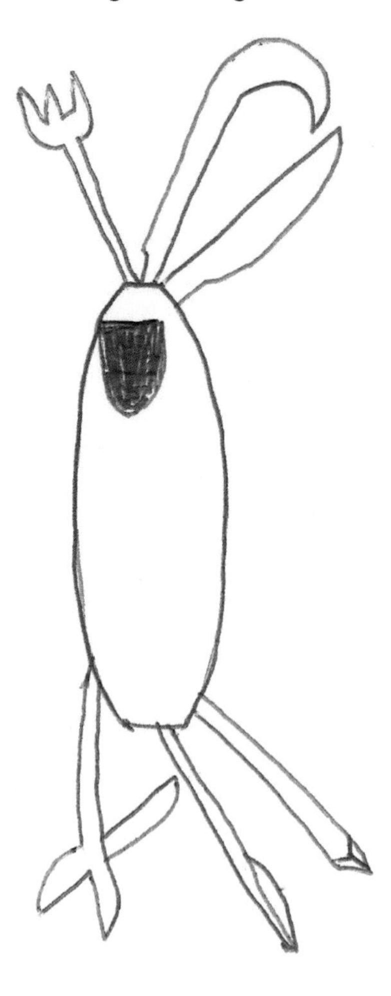

LXXXIII

Viticulturist

Noun [vee-ti-cult-your-ist]

A person who produces artificial vitamins.

Example – Clive had an unusually healthy glow about him, so his manager pulled him into the office and told him being a viticulturist is just like any other job and thieving wouldn't be tolerated.

LXXXIV

Whoremastery

Noun [Horr-mast-er-ee]

A pimp having full control and manipulation over their stable.

Example – Larry was new to the human trafficking game, he didn’t feel he had whoremastery. But for a certain price he knew Callum would help him learn.

Yeoman

Noun [yee-o-mun]

A person who regularly performs charitable acts and tells everyone about it.

Example – Frankie always manages to fit into conversation how many blind people he has trained dogs for. He's such a yeoman, people don't need to know about it as long as it's getting done.

LXXXVI

Zoroastrianism

Noun [Zow-Row-ah-stri-ani-sum]

The notion of purposely copying something, instilled from an ancient race who used to worship a mythological beast, believed to copy the appearance of more dangerous beasts.

Example – Suzie thought it best to get the same shoes and haircut as her classmate Paula, as idea of Zoroastrianism was advised to her by her Nan who used to tuck her into bed at night with the stories passed down from the shapeshifter worshippers. It wasn't until later in life that Suzie realised she had misunderstood her Nan's teachings, which became very apparent as she reflected from her prison cell. There was 3 months left on her sentence for fraud and Suzie knew what she had to do.

LXXXVII

Thanks for Reading!
And thanks to everybody that helped me along the way.

Check out my other works on Instagram:

@The_World_Around_Ewe_Designs

Buy my artwork through my Facebook page:

@TheWorldAroundEwe

47015473R00051

Printed in Poland
by Amazon Fulfillment
Poland Sp. z o.o., Wrocław